ANIMAL TALES

Lucy Kincaid

Illustrated by Eric Kincaid

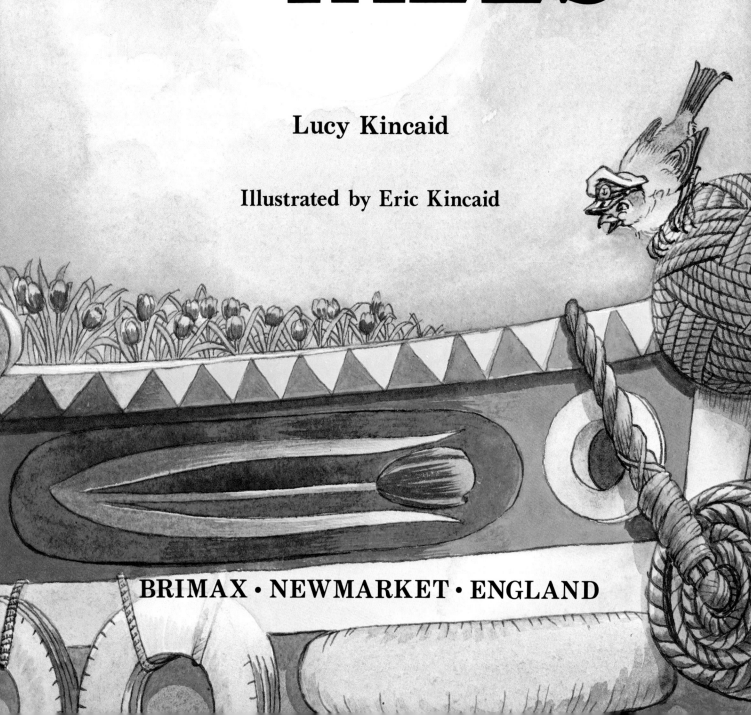

BRIMAX · NEWMARKET · ENGLAND

ISBN 0 86112 300 X
© BRIMAX RIGHTS LTD 1985. All rights reserved
Published by BRIMAX BOOKS, Newmarket, England 1985
This book is an enlarged edition of
'Riverboat Adventures'.
Second printing 1986
Printed in Hong Kong

CONTENTS

Thomas

Wilbur   Minty

HOW IT ALL BEGAN

One fine sunny morning, when Wilbur and his friends were sitting on the riverbank dabbling their feet in the river, Wilbur said, dreamily,

"I've never wanted to sail round the world or anything like that, but I've always thought it would be rather nice to live on a boat."

Minty looked out over the water and sighed deeply. "If only we could," he said. "If only it were possible."

Thomas stopped dabbling his feet and sat very still, as though he suddenly had something very important to think about. Presently he stood up.

"Follow me," he said, and set off at a brisk trot along the riverbank.

"Where are we going?" puffed Wilbur as he and Minty ran after Thomas.

"To see someone I know," said Thomas over his shoulder.

"Is it important?" puffed Minty.

"You'll soon find out," said Thomas mysteriously. He stopped and waited for them at a place where a narrow bridge passed in front of two huge wooden gates.

"Ready?" he asked.

"If we knew what for, we might be able to say," said Minty, but Thomas was already pulling the rope which hung beside the gate. They heard a bell clang somewhere on the other side. Suddenly, a whiskery face appeared over the top of the gate.

"Yes?" said a deep voice. "What do you want?"

"We've come to take a look at the Tulip," said Thomas.

His two friends stared at one another open-mouthed. All that hurrying! Just to look at a tulip!

"Stand where you are!" ordered the voice, "I am the Captain." His whiskery face disappeared. There was the sound of creaking and slowly the gates began to open inwards. Each gate took half the bridge with it, and the half they were standing on took them as well.

"Look at THAT!" gasped Wilbur.

The gates had opened into a narrow inlet, and moored just inside, was a neat little boat once used to fish for herring, but now retired from service at sea. The boat had lace curtains at the wheelhouse windows, shining brass, and flowerpots with red tulips on the deck.

"Is THAT the Tulip?" asked Wilbur, hardly daring to hope.

Minty was speechless. He had fallen in love with the Tulip the moment he had set eyes on her.

13

"Follow me!" said Thomas.

Their knees shaking with excitement, they followed him onto the deck of the Tulip and gazed starry-eyed at everything there was to see.

Presently, Thomas who had been talking to the whiskery old Captain, said, "Well? What do you think?"

"I think she is the most beautiful thing I have ever seen in my life," said Wilbur.

Minty sighed, nodded, and then smiled dreamily. Words were unimportant.

"Well?" said Thomas again. "Shall we?"

"Shall we what?" They didn't understand.

"Have her! You did mean it when you said you would like to live on a boat, didn't you?" For a moment Thomas looked worried. But then, as looks of delight and surprise spread across his friends' faces, he just had to smile.

"Do you mean we can live here, on the Tulip?" whispered Wilbur at last.

"Well, not here exactly. Everything on board is shipshape. She can go out onto the river."

The excitement burst inside Minty like a firework.

"Hooray! Hooray!" he shouted, jumping about as though he had springs tied to his feet. "HOORAY! HOORAY!"

"Look out!" shouted Thomas and dived across the deck to grab hold of Minty. Wilbur got there first, but it was already too late. Minty bounced right over the side, and as Wilbur was holding onto his feet he went over the side too. Suddenly, there he was, in the water, with Minty spluttering and blowing bubbles beside him.

"Help!" cried Minty. "I can't swim! HOORAY! I'm going to live on a boat! Help! HOORAY!"

Wilbur could swim, and he managed to keep Minty afloat until Thomas and the old Captain hooked him out.

15

"If you really are going to live aboard, the first thing you'll have to do is put THAT one in a life jacket," said the old Captain.

"When can we move in?" asked Minty, draped in water weed and beaming like a Cheshire cat. It did not occur to any one that he had just escaped death by drowning.

"Right away if you want to," said the old Captain.

Wilbur was as quick as lightning. He pushed Minty over and sat on him just as he started bouncing again. This time he hiccupped across the deck like a firework that had lost half its fizz, and Thomas and the old Captain managed to anchor him down with brooms before he went over the side again.

"I couldn't help it," said Minty when he had calmed down. "I'm so excited!"

"That's plain to see," said the old Captain.

"I've always wanted to live on a boat myself," said Thomas, "so I know how he feels." To the great astonishment of his friends, who didn't know he could dance, he broke into a sailor's hornpipe that left him breathless with dancing. They watched him, full of admiration.

"I'm glad I'm not coming with you," said the old Captain. "I couldn't stand all that excitement."

"Where are you going?" asked Minty. "You won't be homeless, will you?"

"I've arranged a swop," said Thomas. "The Captain is going to live in my house."

"I've always wanted to live in a house," said the old Captain, a dreamy look coming into his eyes. "And now I've got the chance, so don't you go changing your minds."

"As though we would!" they said.

UNDERWAY

The next few hours were very busy as the old Captain moved his belongings out of the Tulip and the three friends moved in. By the time they had finished, it was almost dark and they were very tired.

Before he went, the old Captain fitted Minty with a life jacket and made him promise to wear it when he was on deck.

"I'll wear it ALL the time," promised Minty.

When the old Captain had waved his final goodbye and disappeared into the shadows along the riverbank path, they went below to the tiny galley and practised how not to tread on each other's toes while they were making cocoa.

Minty took his cocoa into the cabin and climbed into the top bunk before anyone else could claim it.

"I'll drink mine in bed," he said.

In the middle of the night, when everyone was asleep, Minty fell out of the bunk and hit the floor with a bump.

"Are you hurt?" asked Thomas sleepily.

"Of course I'm not," said Minty. "I'm wearing my life jacket."

Thomas and Wilbur were woken a few hours later by a cry for help. Thomas opened one eye and looked at the spot where Minty had landed before. He wasn't there! This time, he was hanging like a yellow moon from the edge of the bunk.

"I was falling out, but then I got caught up," he tried to explain. "I just don't know how it happened."

"That's the best life jacket I've ever seen," said Wilbur. "It's saved your life twice already."

"I think you'd better change places with Wilbur," said Thomas when they had unhooked Minty. "Sooner or later, you're going to hurt yourself."

Minty said he didn't see how, as he was wearing his life jacket. "Life jackets are made to keep you afloat in water, not to give you soft landings," said Thomas.

"You've been lucky so far. What would happen if you fell out head first?" he asked.

"You're right," said Minty and stopped arguing.

They were up so early the next morning even the birds were yawning. They were determined to make an early start. Wilbur was stationed in the wheelhouse. Thomas and Minty took the dinghy and began to tow the Tulip out into the river. The early morning mist lay like a cloud on the water. A small breeze stirred the tops of the trees. The only sounds were the gentle lapping of the water and the creak of the oars.

Suddenly, a voice broke into the quiet, half asleep world, like the crack of a whip. It was very startling. Minty dropped an oar. Thomas gasped.

"You'll never do it. You'll never get THAT out of THERE!"

A fat little frog was standing, with his bicycle, on the towpath.

"Is he talking to us?" asked Minty.

"Of course I'm talking to you," shouted the frog.
"You're heading for disaster! You'll sink the boat! You'll jam the river! You'll hurt yourselves!"

"Ignore him," whispered Thomas. "I know what to do."

"Don't you know ANYTHING about boats?" shouted the frog. "No . . . No . . . NO! You're going too far! You'll ram the bank! Look what you're DOING! Mind that branch! Left a bit . . . No . . . No . . . NO! Back up! Back UP! Never seen such idiots! Shouldn't be left in charge of a boat!"

The frog was turning purple with excitement. If they had listened to what he was shouting and if they had done as he said they should, they would indeed have sunk the Tulip. They would have jammed the river and maybe even drowned. They didn't listen and so none of those things happened.

Soon, piloted by Thomas, the expert, the Tulip was sitting proudly in the middle of the river, with her bow pointing downstream.

"There! I told you that was the way to do it!" shouted the frog, as though it was all his doing. "I'm on the river a lot myself, so I know about these things. Always glad to help anyone in trouble." He gave them a cheery wave, then mounted his bicycle and pedalled off down the towpath. As he rode, his bicycle creaked like a rusty gate and he whistled like an old tin kettle.

"What a cheek," said Wilbur when they were all back on board. "We were never in any trouble."

"We would have been if we had listened to him," said Minty.

"He thought he was being helpful," said Thomas. "Now let's get on with the proper business of the day and get Tulip underway, before he comes back and decides to help us again."

HOOKED

Thomas and Minty were swabbing the deck.

"And a heave and a ho," sang Thomas as he sloshed his mop in the bucket.

"And a ho and a heave," sang Minty as he pushed his mop across the deck.

"Ship ahead!" called Wilbur from the wheelhouse.

Thomas and Minty put down their mops and went to look.

"Better pull over to the bank . . . she's carrying a lot of cargo," said Minty. "It's not very well stowed either. It seems to be moving about. Might cause an accident."

Thomas was looking through a telescope and he smiled to himself. "Better pull over," he called to Wilbur. "It's not the kind of cargo you think it is," he said to Minty.

They all stared in utter amazement as the vessel passed them by. It was crowded from bow to stern with young otters. They were climbing, and clambering, and waving, and jumping, and leaping, and tumbling, and shouting.

"If no one falls overboard it will be a miracle," said Thomas as they disappeared round a bend in the river.

Thomas and Minty had just got the mops back into the buckets when Wilbur called again.

"Something mighty strange ahead!"

"Where?" asked Minty, expecting to see a young otter bobbing about like a cork in the river.

"Up there!" Wilbur pointed to a branch which reached out over the river like an arm with twiggy fingers.

"I can't believe what I'm seeing," said Thomas.

A small figure was hanging from the branch, caught on one of the twigs by the back of its braces. Its arms were waving . . . its legs were waving. Its face was red and cross.

"Get me down! GET ME DOWN!"

"How on earth did you get up there?" called Thomas as Wilbur guided the Tulip till she was directly underneath the branch.

"This horrid tree picked me up!" shouted the little otter. "I wasn't doing anything. I was standing on the cabin roof. And now they've gone without me." Suddenly his face crumpled and he looked as though he was going to cry.

"Were you on that boat?" asked Thomas pointing upstream.

"Yes, I was . . . and I don't like it up here."

Now they understood.

"It's a wonder to me there aren't more of you hanging up there," said Thomas. "Hold still and we'll get you down. Hand me the boathook, Minty."

Thomas pushed the hooked end of the boathook under the otter's braces and carefully lifted him free. He was then faced with a problem. The little otter wasn't dangling from the branch any more, but he WAS dangling from the end of a boathook held straight up in the air.

27

"Put me down! PUT ME DOWN!" cried the otter, flapping about like a bird.

"Keep STILL!" shouted Thomas as he struggled to hold the boathook steady and stop the little otter crashing to the deck.

"Now what do we do?" asked Minty, as Thomas staggered about trying to keep his burden steady.

"I don't know . . . you tell me!" gasped Thomas. "I can't hold him much longer!"

"Get hold of the other side of this!" shouted Wilbur, just behind Minty. "Hurry up!" He was holding a blanket. Just as they got it spread out like a fireman's net, Thomas's arms gave up the struggle. The boathook keeled over. The little otter flew off the end, sailed through the air and landed in the blanket.

He bounced up and down a few times then climbed out and said, "That was fun. I like flying. Let's do that again."

"You're joking, I hope," said Wilbur.

"No, I'm not. I want to do it again. Hook me on." He tried to hook his braces onto the boathook himself.

"Ahoy there!" They had been so busy with the rescue, they hadn't noticed a dinghy pull alongside. "Is that our young 'un you've got there?" a voice called.

"I hope so," said Wilbur. "I don't think we could cope with him for very long."

"We've only just missed him," said the otter in the dinghy. "I came back to look for him."

They breathed sighs of relief as Thomas handed the little otter down to the otter in the dinghy.

"What happened?" they heard him ask as the dinghy moved away. "Did you fall in?"

"Of course I didn't," said the little otter and began to jabber excitedly. "A tree picked me up, and then I went flying. I like flying."

They could still hear his excited little voice when the dinghy had disappeared round the bend in the river. They could hear the other otter saying, "You mustn't make up stories like that. Now tell me what REALLY happened . . . ."

When everything was quiet again, Thomas and Minty finished swabbing the deck. Then they sat and watched the fish plop, the dragonflies flit and Wilbur swim.

"I wonder if we were like that when we were young," said Minty, thinking about the little otters.

"I expect we were," said Thomas.

A MISUNDERSTANDING

There was a seagull flying in circles round the Tulip. Minty was getting dizzy just watching it.

"I don't like the way it's doing that," said Wilbur, who was getting a crick in his neck.

"Look out! Take cover!" shouted Minty. "It's coming down here!"

The seagull landed with a thud on the deck and carefully folded its wings across its back.

"It's BIG!" gasped Minty, and he hid behind a barrel.

"Good afternoon," said Wilbur, standing his ground bravely. "Did you want something?"

The seagull squawked, then stood with its beak open.

"That's not a proper answer," said Wilbur.

"Squawk!" said the seagull, just two inches from Wilbur's nose.

Wilbur backed away, nervously. The seagull advanced. Wilbur stepped, even more nervously, to one side. The seagull stepped in front of him. Whichever way Wilbur stepped, the seagull stepped too. They could have been partners in a barn dance.

"Squawk! Squawk!"

Minty could bear the suspense no longer. He reached out and caught hold of Wilbur's leg. Wilbur fell flat on his face and Minty hauled him behind the barrel.

"You'll be safe here," said Minty.

There was another squawk, this time immediately above their heads. They looked straight up into the wide open beak of the seagull. They had never been so frightened in the whole of their lives.

"THOMAS!" they both shouted, louder than they had ever shouted before. They heard the sound of Thomas's footsteps, and then his voice.

"Hallo! Are you in trouble?"

"C.c.can't you see we are?" they called to him, but Thomas was talking to the seagull, not to them.

"Squawk! Squawk!" said the seagull.

"Yes, of course I will. At once. . . ." they heard Thomas say. They couldn't believe their ears, or their eyes when they peeped from behind the barrel. Thomas's arm was INSIDE the seagull's beak.

Wilbur and Minty were both afraid, but Thomas was their friend, and no seagull was going to eat HIM. They rushed at the seagull and began thumping him with their fists.

"Let him go! Let him go! Do you hear? LET HIM GO!"

"What are you doing?" asked Thomas as calmly as could be, with his arm still inside the seagull's beak.

"Save yourself! Save yourself!" they cried. "Don't let it eat you!"

"Stop it, this instant!" said Thomas sharply.

"You heard what he said! STOP IT!" Wilbur and Minty thumped the seagull so hard that its eyes watered.

"I'm talking to YOU!"
shouted Thomas.

"US?" They were so surprised
they stopped thumping.

"Yes! YOU! Now watch!"
And to their amazement,
Thomas pulled a large fish, tail
first, from the seagull's beak.
"He had that stuck in his
throat. He was asking for help."

"Thank you," said the seagull
as Thomas threw the fish back
into the river. "I couldn't seem
to make your friends
understand."

Wilbur and Minty felt very ashamed and did their best to
smooth the seagull's rumpled feathers. But, as Thomas said
afterwards, it wasn't really their fault. They didn't
understand a seagull's cry for help. There were very few who
did.

DRIFTING

It was the middle of the night.

THUD! THUD! THUD! They ALL heard it. They ALL decided it was the frog being a nuisance again. They ALL put their pillows over their heads and pretended they couldn't hear anything at all. That was a pity, because Tulip had slipped her mooring. As they slept, she drifted downstream like a ghost ship. The frog, who was cycling along the towpath on a midnight mission of his own, saw the trailing rope, guessed what had happened and tried to wake them. He threw clumps of turf at Tulip, and jangled his bicycle bell, but he was wasting his time.

Next morning, Minty woke at the usual time.

"It's very dark this morning," he said to himself. "Perhaps it's raining." He went up on deck to take a look. Two seconds later he was back, shouting,

"Emergency! Emergency! Come quickly!"

Thomas and Wilbur could tell it was important and followed him at once.

"What's happened?" asked Wilbur, looking up at the place where the sky should have been. Instead of blue space and clouds there were sooty black bricks. "Where ARE we?" he asked.

"We seem to be under a bridge," said Thomas.

"But how did we get here?" asked Minty.

Thomas pulled in the loose end of the mooring rope. "That's how," he said. "We must have been drifting all night. And what's worse . . ." he added, looking over the side, "we have run aground on a mud bank."

Wilbur and Minty looked for themselves. Tulip had somehow swung sideways across the river and her bow was firmly wedged in a bank of thick, black mud.

"How did that happen?" asked Minty.

"Because there was nobody in the wheelhouse," sighed Thomas.

"What can we do?" asked Wilbur.

"There is only one thing we can do," said Thomas. "We'll have to pull her off."

Thomas jumped across the gap between the Tulip's stern and the opposite towpath. Wilbur threw him the loose end of the mooring rope and Thomas began to pull. Tulip wouldn't move. She was as stubborn as a mule.

"I'll need some help," called Thomas, Wilbur swung paw over paw down the rope and added his weight to Thomas's. Tulip stayed exactly where she was. She was MORE stubborn than a mule.

Thomas called to Minty. "Get the boathook and try to push her off!" While Minty pushed, and pushed against the side of the bridge, Thomas and Wilbur pulled, and pulled on the rope. Suddenly there was a glucking, sucking noise and Tulip pulled free. Her bow swung round into deep water.

Minty was taken completely by surprise. One moment he was pushing against the wall and the next he was hanging onto the end of the boathook with NOTHING underneath his feet at all. For just the briefest of moments he hovered like a dragonfly, and then, SPLAT! He fell!

When Thomas and Wilbur looked over the side, he was sitting on top of the mud like a little mud pudding with two rather startled eyes staring from it. His life jacket had saved him again.

"Climb out onto the towpath," said Thomas trying to hide a smile, " and we will pick you up further along."

　　As Minty came out from under the bridge there were hoots
of laughter, and shouts of, "Who is that?" "WHAT is that?"
　　"We seem to have collected an audience," sighed Thomas
as he took Tulip out into sunlight and open water.
　　"You'd better get that mud off him before it sets rock hard.
Once it's dry you'll NEVER get it off!"
　　There was a familiar face amongst the others peering over
the parapet.

"I knew you'd get stuck under there. Tricky bit of steering that at the best of times. I've been watching you drift all night," said the frog.

"Then why didn't you warn us?" asked Thomas.

"Oh, but I did" said the frog. "It wasn't my fault you took no notice, was it?" And then they ALL remembered how they had put their pillows over their heads and pretended not to hear anything during the night.

"One thing about living on a boat," said Minty later as Thomas hosed the mud off him, "it's never boring. There's always SOMETHING happening, even if it isn't always what you expect. I'm glad we made the change."

They all were. And they ALL looked forward to lots of tomorrows in which unexpected things would continue to happen.

AHOY THERE!

It was breakfast time aboard the riverboat Tulip.

"There's no jam," said Minty rummaging in the galley larder.

"And no butter," said Wilbur looking inside the butter dish.

"About time we did some shopping then," said Thomas. "I'll make a list if you tell me what we need."

The list was so long when it was finished, Thomas said, "We'll all have to go."

They moored Tulip beside a wooden jetty and set off, carrying empty baskets and bags.

"Are you sure Tulip will be alright on her own?" asked Minty, as they left her lying silently beside the jetty.

"Of course she will," said Thomas. "A bit of peace and quiet will do her good."

They'd been gone for almost an hour when the fat little frog bumped along the jetty on his bicycle and came to a halt alongside Tulip's gangplank.

"Ahoy there! Anyone at home?" he called, his voice sounding even more creaky and squeaky than ever before. It startled the sleeping ducks awake, and they flapped their wings in alarm.

"AHOY THERE! I said, IS ANYONE AT HOME?" called the frog louder still. "CAN ANYONE HEAR ME?" The ducks quacked crossly.

Nothing stirred aboard the Tulip.

"Now, that's very strange," said the frog to himself. "I wonder if they have all been taken ill. Perhaps there has been an accident. Perhaps they have all fallen overboard."

45

The frog propped his bicycle against a post and went, uninvited, up the gangplank. "It's no good waiting to be invited when there is something wrong," he said when the ducks glared at him.

The frog had never been aboard Tulip before, so he didn't know what to expect.

The first thing he did was to trip over a rope and put his foot in a bucket. As he tried to save himself, he shot across the deck with one foot in the bucket and the other foot in the air.

"OW!" he cried as the bucket hit a barrel and he fell out in a heap.

"OUCH!" he cried as his foot twisted under him and he sat on it. "I'll never walk again!" he groaned, leaning over to rub his foot. He sat, just where he had fallen. He waited for someone to come and find him.

The three friends were walking back along the riverbank with loaded bags and baskets. They heard the clatter and the thud as the frog slid across the deck, hit the barrel, and tipped out of the bucket.

"Someone is trying to take Tulip!" shouted Minty. "I knew we shouldn't have left her!" He dropped the baskets he was carrying, not caring that everything spilled out onto the path. He ran towards Tulip, shouting, "STOP THIEF!"

Wilbur dropped his bags and picked up a stout stick. "STOP THIEF!" he shouted, following close on Minty's heels.

"Oh dear," sighed Thomas, as he looked at the scattered shopping. Then he put down his own baskets and ran towards Tulip himself. He wasn't afraid for Tulip because he had seen the frog's bicycle, but he WAS afraid his friends might do something silly.

Minty and Wilbur made so much noise running up the gangplank they frightened the frog. He thought an army was coming aboard to arrest him. Minty and Wilbur had expected to see a gang of pirates, ten at the very least. When they saw the frog sitting in a crumpled heap and hiding his face they were so surprised that they stopped in their tracks.

"Oh . . . it's YOU!" they said.

The frog dared to look up. "Oh . . ." he said, echoing their words. ". . . .it's YOU!"

"What are YOU doing aboard Tulip?" asked Thomas as he came up behind them.

The frog took one look at their cross faces. He told them all they wanted to know, quickly and without fuss. Then, and only then, did he tell them about his fall and his injured foot.

Thomas looked at the frog's foot and prodded it gently.

"There's nothing much wrong with that," he said. "It's only a sprain, but you will have to keep the weight off it for a few days. You'd better stay aboard with us until it's better."

The frog's eyes gleamed with pleasure at the thought.

"Of course, it will be weeks and weeks before I can walk properly," he said. "I won't be any trouble. I promise I won't be any trouble. I'll be so quiet you won't know I'm there."

"I wish I could be sure of that," said Thomas, as he and Minty and Wilbur went to gather up the scattered shopping.

A loud shout followed them along the footpath. "DON'T FORGET TO BRING MY BICYCLE ABOARD! FERGUS FROG GOES NOWHERE WITHOUT HIS BICYCLE!"

"I knew it," sighed Thomas. "He's started telling us what to do already."

Wilbur said, "So that's his name. I've never heard him speak of it before. I didn't think he had one."

49

THE BICYCLE

A week later, Fergus Frog was STILL aboard Tulip. He had sat, every day, with his foot on a box, and with his fishing rod dangling over Tulip's bow. He had done nothing but enjoy the sun, the fishing, and being lazy.

"Fetch me a glass of water!" he called to Minty, who was trying to clean the brass in the wheelhouse.

"Fetch this! Fetch that! Is his foot never going to get better?" grumbled Minty as he filled a glass in the galley.

Fergus took one sip of the water, then handed the glass back to Minty. "Watch my fishing line for a bit," he said.

"Why? What are you going to do?" asked Minty hopefully. "Are you going to test your foot?"

"You know very well it's still very painful," said Fergus. "I'm going to sleep. Wake me in half an hour."

Minty sat and thought sadly how life had changed.

"Since Fergus has been aboard there hasn't been time to do ANYthing properly," he sighed. "If only he'd try to do something for himself. Do you think he's pretending his foot is worse than it really is?"

Thomas, who was passing, didn't answer, but he was beginning to wonder about Fergus himself.

Fergus's bicycle was stowed on deck. He had forbidden anyone to touch it. Now Wilbur looked at Fergus very carefully to make sure he WAS asleep and then he wheeled it out.

51

"You're taking a big risk," said Minty.

"He can't see me . . . he's asleep. And besides, I feel like having some fun," said Wilbur as he mounted the bicycle. "Give me a push."

Either Minty pushed too hard or Wilbur wasn't as clever at riding a bicycle as he thought he was. Maybe it was because his feet didn't reach the pedals. Whatever it was, the bicycle shot across the deck, it scattered everything in its path. The bicycle stopped only after it had thrown Wilbur head over heels into the river.

"Are you alright, Wilbur?" asked Thomas, as he watched Wilbur touch river-bottom and rise up to the surface again.

"Course I am," spluttered Wilbur. "But what's the matter with Fergus?" He could see Fergus's head bobbing up and down beside Thomas as though he was bouncing on a trampoline.

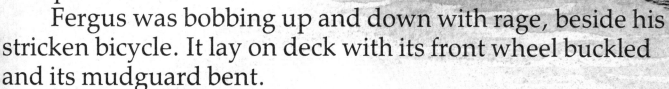

Fergus was bobbing up and down with rage, beside his stricken bicycle. It lay on deck with its front wheel buckled and its mudguard bent.

"How dare you!" shouted Fergus. "How dare you! I told you never to touch my bicycle. Who did it?"

"Doesn't seem to be anything wrong with his foot now," whispered Thomas.

"There's a lot wrong with his temper," said Minty.

Thomas waited till Fergus paused for breath before shouting again, then said, "How's the foot, Fergus?"

"You know how it is! Why do you keep asking? You know I'll never walk properly again!" Fergus was VERY angry.

"You seem to be jumping up and down alright," said Minty. "I wonder why that is."

Fergus didn't have anything to say to that. There was nothing he could say. He just went very red and spluttered a lot. "Well . . . er . . . I . . . er . . . I think I'd better sit down," he said, and hopped back to his seat with his foot hanging limply, as though all the bones in it had turned to jelly.

"And put my bicycle back where it belongs," he called over his shoulder sadly.

"A bicycle can't really be that hard to ride," said Wilbur as he picked it up from the deck. "I'm going to have another try."

Fergus jumped from his chair, shot across the deck as though he was propelled by a rocket. He snatched his bicycle from Wilbur.

"Leave my bicycle alone!" he shouted. "I'm not staying here a minute longer! I'm leaving and I'm taking my bicycle with me!"

"But what about your poor injured foot," said Thomas. "You said yourself it was . . ."

"There's nothing wrong with my foot! LET ME OFF!!!"

What a relief it was to them all to see Fergus Frog pedalling off down the towpath. A bit wobbly, maybe, but that was due to the bent bicycle wheel and had nothing to do with his foot.

"What a nerve he's got," said Minty.

"Will someone sit me down. I feel tired," said Thomas without the trace of a smile.

Wilbur and Minty looked at him, and at each other for just one second before they jumped on him.

"I give in!" laughed Thomas, as he held them off. "I was only joking."

THE LOCK-KEEPER'S WIFE

There had been a line of boats waiting to go through the lock all afternoon, and now Tulip had joined it.

"What's the hold-up?" called Thomas to the boat in front.

"Waiting for the lock-keeper," someone said.

"Where is he?"

"His wife has locked him in the lodge."

"Can't someone let him out?"

"No, his wife has the key."

In the distance, for the line was a long one, they could just see the lock-keeper's whiskery face pressed against the lodge window.

"Perhaps someone should do something," said Thomas. When no one moved, Thomas said, "Perhaps we should do something ourselves." He pushed unwilling Wilbur and Minty ashore and they went up to the lodge.

"Can't you get through the window?" shouted Thomas as loudly as he could. The poor lock-keeper shook his head.

"I'm too fat," he said.

"Why did she lock you in?" asked Thomas.

"All I said was, 'Where are the blackberries in the blackberry pie?' and she hit me with the rolling pin, then ran out of the house and locked me in."

"Where is she now?"

"Standing guard at the back door."

"We'll go and talk to her."

"Has she still got the rolling pin?" asked Wilbur.

"She has," said the lock-keeper. "So be careful."

Everyone watched as they went round to the back of the house. They soon saw why no one had done anything. The lock-keeper's wife was standing guard with her rolling pin ready. She was very plump and almost as whiskery as the lock-keeper himself.

"Doesn't she look fierce," whispered Minty.

"Who are you? What do you want? And NO I WON'T!" Her voice was as spiky as a prickly hedge in winter.

"She's still angry," whispered Thomas.

"Of course I'm angry," she replied. Her ears were as sharp as an owl's. "It's not my fault the birds ate most of the blackberries, but you'd think it was, the way he shouts at me."

"Please, let him out so that we can get through the lock," said Minty.

"No I won't. Not until he says he is sorry."

"How can he if he's locked in?"

"That's his problem."

59

"It's our problem if we are to get through the lock today," whispered Thomas quietly. Even Wilbur didn't hear him, and he was standing right beside him.

"She could always put an apple in it," said Wilbur.

"An apple in what?" asked Minty.

"The pie. Blackberries and apples go well together in a pie."

The lock-keeper's wife heard that too. "He'll get no blackberry and apple pie from me," she said.

"Don't suppose she knows how to make one," whispered Minty, not quietly enough because the lock-keeper's wife went very red. Minty thought for one moment that he was going to be rolled out like a piece of pastry.

"I'll show you whether I can make a blackberry and apple pie, or not!" she said.

She picked two apples from the nearest tree and marched round to the front of the lodge, with Thomas and Minty following at a safe distance behind.

Wilbur ran ahead to warn the lock-keeper.

"Look out!" he said, "She's coming! Try to slip through, when she unlocks the door!"

The lock-keeper's wife took the key from her apron pocket. Her hands were already full with the apples and the rolling pin. She dropped the key.

Wilbur dived between her legs and picked it up.

"I'll unlock the door for you," he said. He made a sign to the lock-keeper to be ready.

The lock-keeper was out . . . the lock-keeper's wife was in . . . and the key turned again, in the twinkling of an eye. The lock-keeper's wife didn't hear the cheers that came from the long line of waiting boats. She marched straight to the kitchen. "I'll show them whether I can make a blackberry and apple pie, or not," she said.

Rolling pastry and baking always soothed her temper when it went right, and this time it did. By the time it was Tulip's turn to go through the lock, she was putting the pie to cool and she had a smile on her face.

"For goodness sake, say something nice about the pie,"
called Thomas softly, as Tulip slipped past the lock-keeper.
"Don't worry. I've learnt my lesson," said the lock-keeper,
and then added, with a wink, "I think it's safe to unlock the
door now, don't you?"

THE RACE

The sun was shining. A gentle breeze was blowing. Wilbur was lying on his back, watching small white clouds drift across the sky, like little woolly lambs. Minty was lying with a handkerchief over his face. Thomas had found a place in the shade and was studying the map.

Presently Minty sat up. "What's that twittering noise?" he said.

Thomas and Wilbur listened. There was a twittering noise. It seemed to be coming from the river. Thomas left his map and went to look. The twittering stopped.

"Hallo!" the others heard him say, with surprise in his voice.

"Who is it?" asked Minty.

"Come and look for yourself," smiled Thomas.

They had moored Tulip close to a cluster of lily pads. Every lily pad was covered with small frogs. They were very small frogs, the largest was no bigger than a walnut.

"What's going on?" whispered Minty.

"Where have they all come from?"

"What are they doing?"

"Please sir, we're going to have a swimming race," said one of the frogs.

The twittering broke out again. "He's here . . . he's here . . ." twittered the excited little voices. "Fergus is here . . ."

"Fergus? What has Fergus got to do with all this?"

It was a good question.

Fergus was on the towpath with his bicycle and a loud hailer.

"Get ready!" he called, through the hailer, and added, without giving anyone time to get ready,

"READYSTEADYGO!"

Not one of the frogs was ready. None were steady. But they all went.

There were plips, and plops and splashes in all directions.

"I always thought," said Wilbur to Thomas, "that in a race everyone went in the same direction."

"So they do," said Thomas.

"Then why aren't they?" Thomas's reply was drowned in the sound of Fergus's voice booming through the hailer.

"What do you think you're doing you silly little frogs! YOU ARE ALL GOING THE WRONG WAY!!!!!"

At once, all the frogs did a turn-over flip and swam off in a different direction.

"He's confusing the poor little things," said Wilbur as the river churned and bubbled, like water in a witch's cauldron.

"Stop! You silly little frogs!" stormed Fergus.

The frogs stopped swimming and began to tread water. They were trying to do the right thing. The trouble was, they just didn't know what was the right thing to do. They were getting muddled. Some of the smaller ones were getting tearful.

"Can't you do something, Thomas?" whispered Wilbur.

"I think I'd better," said Thomas. "Cover your ears because I'm going to shout."

"FERGUS!" Thomas shouted so loudly he hurt his throat. Fergus was so startled he fell off his bicycle. The frogs were so startled they bobbed underwater, so that only their eyes were showing.

"FERGUS! COME HERE!!!"

Wilbur and Minty had never seen Thomas look so commanding before. They were very impressed.

Fergus picked himself up and came without a sound.

"Yes? What do you want?" he asked meekly.

"Give me that hailer. I'll start the race!"

Fergus handed it over without a word. No one would have dared disobey Thomas when he spoke like that.

Thomas soon had the frogs all ready. He lined them up on lily pads right across the river. He sent Fergus to stand half a mile upstream. "You're the winning post," he said.

"Nobody moves until I shout go," he explained to the eager little frogs. "The first one past Fergus is the winner."
"READY!   STEADY!   GO!!!!!!"

What a race it was. Minty and Wilbur cheered till they were hoarse. Thomas lost his voice completely. Fergus went purple with delight. "Come on! Come on!" he yelled. "I'll take the winner for a ride on my bicycle!"

Fergus kept his word. He wheeled the winner all the way back along the riverbank. No one minded losing. Everyone had enjoyed the swim too much.

"That was exciting," sighed Wilbur.

"I don't know when I've enjoyed myself so much," said Minty.

Thomas wanted to say, 'Hear, hear!' but he had to wait for his voice to come back. By the time it did, everyone else had found a place to lie in the shade and was fast asleep.

"It was exciting," said Thomas as he looked at all the sleeping frogs, and at Wilbur and Minty asleep with smiles on their faces. "It was exciting . . . but then, living on the river is exciting all the time."

LOST AND FOUND

One sunny morning, the Riverboat Tulip was chugging downstream, with Thomas singing songs in the wheelhouse and with Minty and Wilbur leaning over the side watching the riverbank slide by. Then they spotted Fergus Frog. He was on the bank his bicycle beside him. Water was running from his back and creating a pool around him.

"Hallo, Fergus!" called Minty cheerfully.

Fergus looked up and gave a sad, limp wave. He looked very glum indeed.

Thomas shut off the engine and came down from the wheelhouse. "What's the matter?" he asked. "Is something wrong?"

Fergus nodded sadly.

"What is the matter then?" asked Thomas, wishing Fergus would say something. Fergus was not behaving at all like himself.

"I've lost my bicycle bell," sighed Fergus.

"Lost it? How?" asked Thomas.

"It fell off my bicycle and rolled into the river."

"Then dive in and get it," said Minty.

"What do you think I've been doing?" said Fergus, with a flash of his old spirit. "Why do you think I'm wet? I've been diving all morning . . . I'm water-logged . . . I'm tired . . . I've got cramp . . . and now my legs have forgotten how to swim."

"That's impossible," said Minty, whose legs couldn't swim at all.

"No it's not!" snapped
Fergus. He tried to stand, but
his legs buckled beneath him
and he folded up into an untidy
heap on the ground.

Wilbur looked at Fergus's
woebegone face, and found
himself saying, "Now don't you
worry. I'll get it for you."

There was hardly a ripple as
Wilbur dived down into the
river. Minty couldn't help
sighing. If only he could do that.

"Your troubles are over,"
called Minty. "Wilbur is an
expert. He'll find your bell in no
time."

"I don't see how, if I can't. I'm
an expert too, you know,"
grumbled Fergus.

"Just you wait and see," said
Minty.

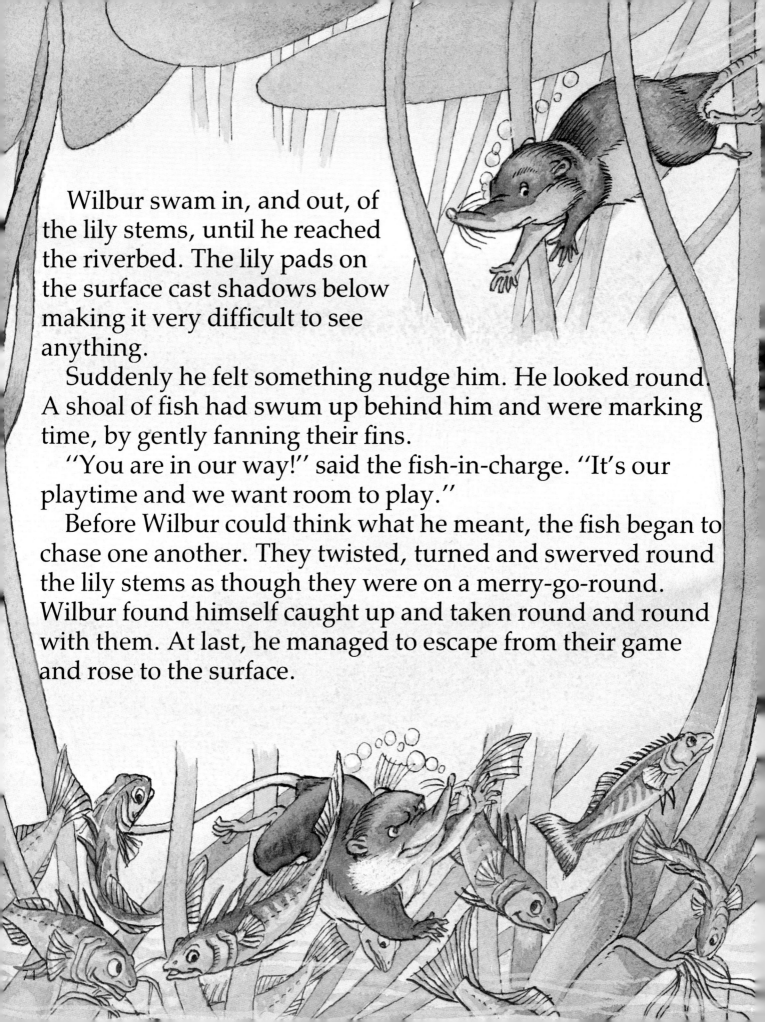

Wilbur swam in, and out, of the lily stems, until he reached the riverbed. The lily pads on the surface cast shadows below making it very difficult to see anything.

Suddenly he felt something nudge him. He looked round. A shoal of fish had swum up behind him and were marking time, by gently fanning their fins.

"You are in our way!" said the fish-in-charge. "It's our playtime and we want room to play."

Before Wilbur could think what he meant, the fish began to chase one another. They twisted, turned and swerved round the lily stems as though they were on a merry-go-round. Wilbur found himself caught up and taken round and round with them. At last, he managed to escape from their game and rose to the surface.

"Have you found it?" asked Minty eagerly.

"No!" gasped Wilbur, taking a big gulp of air, and feeling just a bit giddy. "The fish are out at play."

"Go back! GO BACK!" shouted Fergus in a panic. "They will churn up the mud and bury my bell and then it will be lost forever!" He tried to dive in himself, but Thomas who had gone ashore to massage the frog's cramped legs, held him back.

"Leave it to Wilbur," Thomas said. "It's dangerous to swim when you've got cramp." He was much bigger than Fergus, so Fergus had to do as he was told.

"Go back! Go back!" shouted Fergus, struggling hard, but in vain, to get past Thomas. "GO BACK BEFORE IT'S TOO LATE!"

Wilbur took a deep breath. He dived, as swift and straight as an arrow, and reached the riverbed before the fish could pull him into their game. He had to swim very close to the bottom to keep out of their way. His whiskers kept puffing up the mud into little murky clouds.

Minty was watching from Tulip. He could see the fish playing. He could see the clouds of mud as Wilbur was forced closer and closer to the bottom.

"Do something, Thomas!" he called. "Or we will lose Wilbur as well!"

"Yes, Thomas! DO something!" added Fergus. "Do something about those fish!"

Thomas thought for a moment, then called loudly across the water, "IT'S STORY TIME!"

"STORY TIME!" Fergus nearly exploded. "I meant do something SENSIBLE! Story time indeed!"

Now Thomas knew the fish better than Fergus did. They came with a rush, and listened spellbound as Thomas told them a story about pirates and sunken treasure.

Wilbur was able to carry on the search unhindered. He found the bell at last, and only just in time. It was already half buried in the mud. He carried it up to the surface and held it high so that everyone could see it.

"GOT IT!" he cried.

"Shush!" said Fergus rudely. "Can't you see we're listening to a story!"

"Well, of all the cheek!" gasped Wilbur. "There's thanks for you!"

"Never mind him," whispered Minty. "I think you're clever, and Fergus will be pleased when he has finished listening. Thomas always tells a good story. You know that."

It was true. Thomas did and Minty was right about Fergus. When the story was finished he came and said 'thank you'. He really meant it, of course, and was very pleased.

THE TUNNEL

"Tunnel ahead!" called Wilbur, one morning.

Thomas stopped Tulip and they all went ashore to take a look at what lay ahead. They stood on the towpath and peered into a long sleeve of darkness. They could just about see a tiny spot of light, far off in the distance.

"It's long," said Minty, gulping.

"Not much headroom either," said Thomas, looking up at its roof. "We'd better lower the mast."

"Will it be dangerous?" asked Minty nervously.

"I shouldn't think so," said Thomas.

78

As soon as they had lowered the mast, they began to ease Tulip forward into the tunnel. The further in they went the darker it got. They lit all the lanterns they could find and placed them round the deck.

"It's as dark as night in here," said Minty. 'IT'S AS DARK AS NIGHT IN HERE' said his echo loudly, startling them all.

"We'd better whisper," said Thomas softly. "Everything sounds louder in a tunnel. We don't want to frighten anyone who lives in here, do we?"

"I suppose not," said Minty nervously, wondering what kind of creatures lived in tunnels. He hoped they were not big ones . . . or dangerous ones. For the first time he noticed eyes watching them from ahead of the tunnel.

"It's a monster!" cried Minty in a panic. "Look at its fiery eyes! It's going to swallow us up! What shall we do?" He began to jump about like a firework.

"Don't be silly," laughed Thomas. "It's another boat. Those eyes are lanterns."

"Oh," said Minty, "that's all right then."

"No it isn't!" cried Wilbur. It was his turn to panic. "They'll never see us in the dark . . . we'll have a collision!"

"SHOUT!" cried Minty. He and Wilbur began to shout at the tops of their voices. As well as shouting, they kicked, shook, and banged anything that would clang, rattle or ring. The noise inside that tunnel was just deafening.

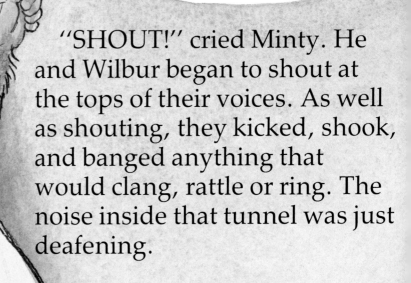

"Stop!" cried Thomas, pulling his hat over his ears in an effort to keep the noise out of his head. "If we can see their lights . . . they can see ours . . . For goodness sake stop shouting before you deafen me."

But Wilbur and Minty either couldn't, or didn't want to hear. They went on shouting, banging, thumping and yelling as though their very lives depended on it. There was only one thing left to do. Thomas did it. He picked them up, one under each arm, and carried them, still yelling fit to burst, across the deck, and bundled them below.

Before they realised what had happened, the door was slammed shut and two heavy barrels were rolled against it. They couldn't open it, no matter how hard they tried.

It didn't stop them shouting, yelling, banging and thumping. At least it muffled the sound a bit so that Thomas could hear himself think.

Tulip passed the other boat with only inches to spare. It took all of Thomas's skill to stop them bumping. He was thankful Minty and Wilbur weren't beside him jogging his elbow.

They had their faces pressed hard against one of the portholes, silent at last, hardly daring to breathe as the other boat slipped past them like a large black shadow.

"What was all that noise about?" called someone from the other boat.

"Oh . . . er . . . nothing . . . everything under control," said Thomas, wishing they hadn't asked.

"Thought the roof must have fallen in at the very least," shouted the voice as it was swallowed up in the darkness.

Thomas didn't roll back the barrels and let Minty and Wilbur out until Tulip was safely through the tunnel.

"Why did you do that?" asked Wilbur.

"I thought it would be safer," said Thomas, though he didn't say why.

Minty rubbed his eyes in the bright sunshine and looked back at the tunnel.

"Are you sure it wasn't a monster?" he asked.

"Of course it wasn't," laughed Thomas. "Now make yourself useful, and help me get the mast up."

Wilbur was swallowing carefully. "I don't think tunnels agree with me," he said. "It must be the air, or something . . . my throat feels quite sore."

"That's funny," said Minty. "So does mine. I wonder why?"

"Is yours all right, Thomas?" asked Wilbur.

"Yes," said Thomas. "Mine is perfectly all right."

They didn't see him smile to himself as he went to fetch something to make their sore throats better. He could have told them why they had sore throats but he decided to say nothing.

OVERLAND RESCUE

"What are we going to do today?" asked Wilbur.

Thomas didn't answer, he was looking at something through the telescope.

"Take a look," he said, handing the telescope to Wilbur.

"I wonder how that happened?" said Wilbur.

"What are you looking at?" asked Minty, and took the telescope to see for himself.

"Poor little thing," he said. "I hope someone rescues him."

But nobody did. Ten minutes later the little dormouse was still hanging upside down in the brambles.

"Don't look so worried," said Wilbur, as Minty's face creased with worry lines. "We'll go and rescue him ourselves."

Thomas would have gone too had he known they were going. However they were in too much of a hurry to stop and tell him. The first he knew was when he looked through the telescope to see if the dormouse had been rescued. He saw Minty and Wilbur running across the fields. He swung the telescope round to see if there was anyone else about. Fergus Frog was pedalling along the leafy path on his bicycle.

Fergus could not see Minty and Wilbur. Minty and Wilbur could not see Fergus. There was going to be an accident. Thomas could see them all and knew that it was bound to happen, but there was nothing he could do to stop it. They were too far away to hear his shouts. So he stood and watched it all happen through the telescope.

They collided, as Thomas knew they would, where the footpath across the field, and the path alongside the hedge met.

"What are you doing here? Why aren't you on the river?" demanded Fergus crossly as they all sat rubbing their bruises and making sure they had no broken bones.

"There's a dormouse caught in a bramble bush. We're rescuing him," said Wilbur.

"Looks like it, I must say," sniffed Fergus.

"Take no notice of him," said Wilbur as he helped Minty to his feet. They set off again without a backward glance.

"Wait for me!" called Fergus. "I'll come and help."

He jumped onto his bicycle and pedalled after them.

"Hold onto the saddle," he said as he drew level with them, "I'll give you a tow."

Thomas of course, was still watching through the telescope. He laughed until his sides ached at the sight of Fergus and his bicycle bumping up and down across the field. Wilbur and Minty were hanging onto the back of the saddle, running for all they were worth, with their feet hardly touching the ground.

Wilbur and Minty reached the bramble patch quite out of breath with the distinct feeling that they had been flying.

The little dormouse was still hanging upside down. He was crying helplessly. "I thought no one was ever going to come," he wailed when he saw them, the tears streaking his face. "I thought I was going to be caught here for ever and ever and ever and . . ."

"That's long enough," interrupted Fergus. "How did you get up there in the first place?"

"I don't rightly know," sobbed the dormouse.

"Typical!" said Fergus. "I've never yet met a dormouse who knew what he was doing. Dozy things, dormice."

It began to look as though the dormouse was going to be stuck in the brambles for ever. None of them could reach up high enough to lift him free.

"You'll just have to stay there till the wind blows you down," said Fergus.

"Shush!" whispered Minty as the dormouse howled loudly. "Don't say things like that. Can't you see he's upset enough already. If only Thomas were here. He would know what to do."

"I know what to do," said Wilbur. "We'll use Fergus's bicycle."

"Oh no, you won't!" said Fergus, ignoring the dormouse's tears, which were plopping on his head like raindrops.

"Let me finish what I'm about to say before you start arguing," said Wilbur. "You have got the longest legs so you can reach higher than anyone else."

"I know that. But I've tried, haven't I? You've seen me, haven't you? And I couldn't reach, could I?" Fergus was getting cross.

"You could if you stood on your bicycle saddle," said Wilbur, ignoring Fergus's scowl.

"And how am I going to do that? I'm not an acrobat you know," said Fergus. "And my bicycle doesn't stand up by itself either."

"We can hold it for you," said Wilbur.

"Of course we can," said Minty. "We're very good at holding things."

"How do I know I can trust you?" said Fergus.

"Oh, please do," wailed the little dormouse between his sobs.

"Please . . ." said Minty and Wilbur together. "We know you can do it."

"Oh very well," grumbled Fergus. "But hold it steady."

Minty and Wilbur stood one on either side of the bicycle and held it steady. Fergus climbed onto the saddle. After a lot of dithering and wobbling he managed to stand up and nearly got down again when he pricked himself. Minty and Wilbur said if he dared to, they would tip him and his bicycle into the middle of the brambles.

Fergus stretched up, and up, till his long legs looked like tightly stretched elastic. He could just reach.

He unhooked the dormouse . . . the dormouse, of course, couldn't help himself and fell down on top of Fergus. Fergus in turn fell on top of Wilbur and Minty. They had no choice but to let go of the bicycle. Down they all fell to the ground in a tangled heap . . . the bicycle on top. No one knew quite just how it all happened.

They picked themselves up and wiped away the little dormouse's tears. When they had seen him to his door they went back to Tulip. Fergus went with them.

"You'll never guess what happened," said Fergus as Thomas came to meet them.

"I don't need to guess, I know!" said Thomas patting the telescope. "I watched it all as it happened. It was a very fine rescue, even though things didn't go quite according to plan. I'm proud of you all."

BEAVERS

Thomas was leaning over the side of Tulip looking at the river.

"There's something happening down there," he said. "The fish are behaving very strangely."

The fish had gathered together in a large crowd. Their fins were flapping nervously and they were all talking at once. "What's happening? What's happening?" they were saying. "The river is rising . . . what's happening?"

"Is there going to be a flood?" asked Minty, making sure all the fastenings on his life jacket were done up.

"I hope not," said Thomas. "I don't see why there should be. There isn't a cloud in the sky."

"Perhaps the fish are making a fuss about nothing," said Wilbur hopefully.

"They don't usually," said Thomas.

93

"What's that?" asked Wilbur a little later, as they swung round a bend in the river. Someone had built a dam of logs and branches across the river. The river was lapping against it, trying to push it out of the way. The dam was stronger than the river and wouldn't let any water pass and that was why the river was rising.

"It's a dam," said Thomas.

"But who put it there?" asked Wilbur.

"There are the culprits," said Thomas pointing to the bank, where a group of young beavers were rolling a log towards the river.

"HEY!" shouted Thomas. "STOP THAT! STOP IT I SAY!"

The busy little beavers took no notice. They rolled the log into the water and paddled it towards the dam.

"That's clever," said Minty.

"Clever it may be," said Thomas, "but they shouldn't be doing it. This is serious. They've got to be stopped."

Help was already at hand. Fergus had ridden along that way earlier and had seen the little beavers at work. He too had shouted at them to stop, but they had taken no notice of him. So off he had gone in search of their parents.

Father Beaver came panting through the trees, looking very flustered with Mother Beaver and Fergus not far behind.

"Oh dear! Oh dear!" he was saying. "Those naughty children. They know they shouldn't build there. I do wish they would pay attention to what I say. Children! CHILDREN!" He demanded that his children stop what they were doing and listen to him. He might just as well have been talking to himself.

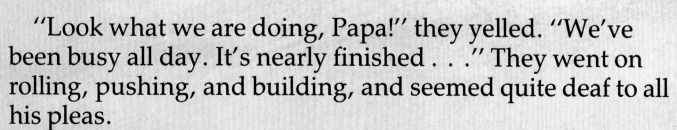

"Look what we are doing, Papa!" they yelled. "We've been busy all day. It's nearly finished . . ." They went on rolling, pushing, and building, and seemed quite deaf to all his pleas.

"Listen to what your father is telling you!" shouted Fergus. "I always listen to what my father says!"

Father Beaver swam out into the river and climbed onto the dam. He put on his sternest expression. He was a kindly old beaver and he found that difficult.

"Now just you listen to me," he said sternly. "I've told you a hundred times NOT to practise building dams in the river. It's the wrong place to practise. Do you hear me? The WRONG place! The river will flood and then we will all be in trouble. How many more times must I tell you? You must check with me first before you start building!"

This time the little beavers couldn't help but hear him. They looked so crestfallen, Minty felt quite sorry for them.

"They are only babies. They don't know any better," he said.

Thomas sighed. "That may be so, but there's a time and a place for everything. This is neither the time nor the place to build a dam."

"It will have to be moved," said Father Beaver sternly. "There will be no supper until every branch and every log is back on dry land."

"They'll never be able to do it on their own before nightfall," said Thomas. "We'll have to help. Come on, Wilbur."

"I wish I could swim," sighed Minty. "Then I could help." Minty was very sad when the little beavers had been stopped building by their father. The little beavers however, had cheered up. They soon discovered it was just as much fun rolling logs out of the river as it was rolling them into the river. Poor Minty sat alone and forlorn. He grew more and more miserable.

"Don't sit there feeling sorry for yourself!" shouted Fergus as he rolled a log along with his webbed feet. "Make yourself useful. Go and pull the logs out of the water as we bring them to you."

Minty jumped up eagerly. "Yes . . . yes . . . I will . . . straight away . . ." he shouted happily. He hurried ashore and as each log touched the bank he pulled it out of the water.

Once he leant over too far and fell in. He was rescued by one of the little beavers.

"It's a good thing I am wearing my life jacket," said Minty as the little beaver pushed him up onto the bank.

"Is that what it is?" said the little beaver cheekily. "I thought you had fallen into a pot of paint."

Just as the sun was setting the last log was rolled up onto the bank, and the river returned to its right level. Mother Beaver took the little beavers home to give them supper and put them to bed. Father Beaver said he was sorry for all the trouble his young ones had caused.

"No harm done," said Thomas as they sat on the bank round the campfire. "To tell you the truth, I've quite enjoyed myself . . . but don't let them do it again. Now did you ever hear the story about . . ." And so ended a rather eventful day.

SWIMMING LESSON

"Will you teach me to swim?" said Minty the day after they had taken the beavers' dam apart.

Wilbur and Thomas were playing in one of the riverside pools. They were swimming on their backs, and diving, turning somersaults, and picking up pebbles with their toes. All Minty could do was sit on the bank and dabble his toes in the water.

"I never get wet all over," he sighed.

"Well, hardly ever," laughed Thomas.

"You'll have to take that life jacket off," said Wilbur.

Minty unbuckled it and dropped it on to the grass.

"He means it," said Wilbur, looking very surprised indeed. "He really does want to learn how to swim."

"Then we must do our best to teach him," said Thomas.

They found a place where the water was shallow and Minty waded in.

"Hold onto me, don't let me go . . . I can't swim yet," he said. "This is far enough," he said when the water lapped his tummy. He leant forward until his chin touched the water. Thomas held him round the middle so that he couldn't sink.

"Take your feet off the bottom," said Wilbur. Just to make sure Minty did, Wilbur went down and lifted them off the bottom himself. Then he bobbed up and showed Minty what to do with his legs. Minty began to kick.

"I'm swimming!" he cried. He forgot his chin was touching the water and in his excitement swallowed a mouthful. "Let me go! I want to do it by myself."

"I'm not sure that I should," said Thomas.

"Please . . . let me go . . . I want to do it by myself," said Minty. So Thomas let go. Minty sank like a stone.

"What happened?" he spluttered as Thomas lifted him out of the water.

"I let go as you asked, and you sank," said Thomas.

"It must have been a mistake . . . I'll try again," said Minty bravely.

During the course of the next hour, Minty sank to the bottom like a stone so many times he could do it with his eyes open without getting frightened.

"It's no good," said Thomas as he hauled Minty out for the umpteenth time. "You've just got to admit that you will never be able to swim. It must be your shape."

"But I want to play in the water with you and Wilbur," said Minty. "You have so much fun. It's no fun for me, just watching."

"Perhaps he could swim with his life jacket on," said Wilbur. "At least he wouldn't sink with it on."

"Let me try!" said Minty eagerly, and buckled himself back into his life jacket.

Thomas and Wilbur led him again into the water. He'd only gone a few steps when he felt the water lift him off his feet.

"I'm floating! I'm floating!" he cried. "Let me go!"

Thomas and Wilbur did just that and waited to see what would happen. The only thing they were sure of was that Minty wouldn't sink. He began to bob about like a cork.

"Look at me!" he cried. "I'm floating!"

"Kick your legs!" said Thomas.

Minty made a tremendous splash, and for some reason, he began to turn round in a circle.

"How is he doing that?" asked Wilbur in amazement.

"If only we knew, we could do it too," laughed Thomas.

"I'm swimming! I'm swimming!" cried Minty, turning round and round and round, in a flurry of splashes.

"That's not what I call swimming," laughed Thomas. "That's what I call bobbing!"

"I don't mind what you call it," said Minty, "because now I can play too."

Thomas and Wilbur pretended Minty was a big yellow ball. They pushed him backwards and forwards, and dived under him, and pushed him upwards and over so that he turned somersaults. He even picked up pebbles with his toes, though Thomas had to hold him down before he could do that.

Minty knew he wasn't swimming properly, but it didn't matter. "If you can't swim," he said to everyone, "then the next best thing is bobbing."

CARGO

Minty and Wilbur had spent the morning making everything spick and span. They had put away the mops and buckets and were laughing at their faces in the shining brass when Thomas pointed to the riverbank.

"It looks as though someone is in trouble," he said.

A cart, laden with furniture and packing cases, had lost a wheel and was leaning over crazily to one side. Around it, and on top of it, and all over it, were a family of mice trying to rescue things as they slid, slowly but surely, to the ground.

They went ashore to see if they could help. The wheel of the cart had hit a rock and was badly broken. It would have to be repaired before it could be put back.

"You won't be going far today," said Thomas.

Mother Mouse threw her apron over her head and wailed. All the mice children ran and clutched at her skirts.

"I don't know what we are going to do," said Father Mouse sadly.

"Were you going far?" asked Wilbur.

"Two miles down river," said Father Mouse. "We must move into our new house today or we will lose it."

"Eeek . . . Eeek . . ." squeaked all the mice children and the mouse mother together. "Eeek . . . Eeek . . ."

Thomas took Wilbur and Minty to one side. "We've got to help," he said.

"How?" asked Minty. "We haven't got a wheel."

"And we can't carry all that furniture for two miles," said Wilbur.

"That's true," said Thomas. "But Tulip can."

Wilbur and Minty helped the mice carry everything aboard. Thomas stowed it properly so that it wouldn't move about and get damaged on the journey. They even found room for the cart and its broken wheel.

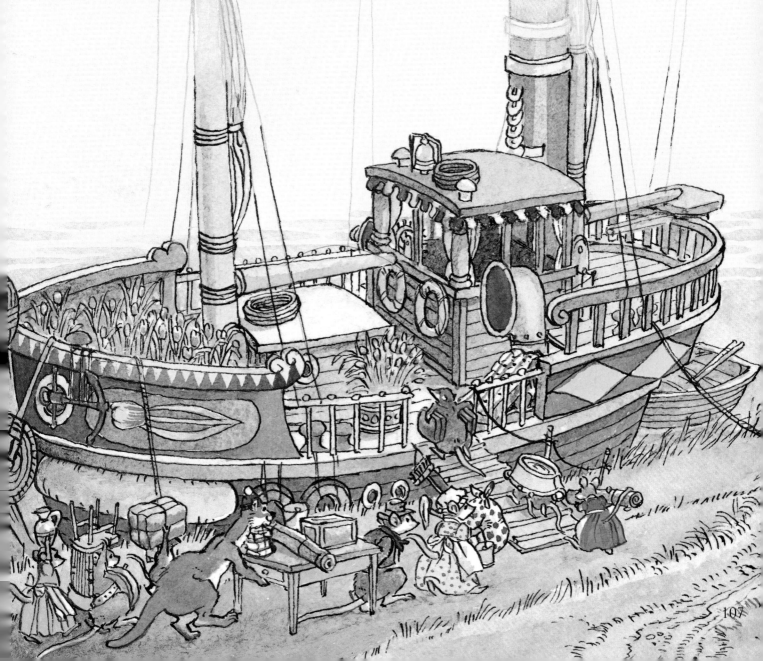

At last everything was safely aboard, and they were ready to pull up the gangplank. The mouse family lined up along the bank to wave them off.

"How are you going to get yourselves to the new house?" asked Thomas.

"Oh, we'll walk," they said cheerfully. "We are used to walking. We walk everywhere."

Thomas looked at Wilbur and Minty as though he was asking them a question. They nodded, as though they were giving him an answer.

"We'll take you as well," said Thomas.

"HURRAH! HURRAH!" shouted the mice children.

"Look out!" shouted Wilbur, jumping on top of a packing case. He pulled Minty after him, as the mice children rushed aboard all together.

When they had got over their excitement, the little mice sat in a row on a rolled up carpet. They chattered and squeaked excitedly, but they didn't move at all. Father Mouse stood in the wheelhouse. He was so proud he couldn't stop his ears twitching and his hat kept falling over his eyes. Mother Mouse sat on one of the chairs and waved to everyone they passed.

They all waved to Fergus. He was so surprised he just stood and stared. For once, although he had his mouth wide open and looked as though he wanted to say something, not a word came out.

Later that evening, the last piece of furniture and the last packing case had been unloaded and carried into the new mouse home. The mice had waved goodbye, the three friends had supper and went to bed. They were very, very tired, but they were happy too.

"There's never a dull moment on the river, is there?" yawned Minty, before he closed his eyes.

"If there is, we've never seen it," yawned Wilbur, after he had closed his eyes.

"I don't suppose we ever will," yawned Thomas as he turned down the wick in the lantern.

A SCARE!

All was quiet aboard the Riverboat Tulip. Everyone had had a busy morning, and now they were lazing in the sun. Thomas was reading. Minty and Wilbur had been playing games, but now they had both fallen asleep. None of them saw the towel, which Minty had pegged out to dry, slip from its pegs and glide away with the breeze.

None of them saw it waft down gently and cover a duck who was sleeping in the reeds.

"Quack!" squawked the duck as she found herself trapped in something thick and white. "Quuuaaack!!!" She opened her wings and tried to shake it off. It wouldn't move.

"Quuuaaack!!!" she squawked again, and plunged with wings fluttering, through the reeds and into the river.

Minty heard the noise and went to find out what was happening. He staggered back across the deck.

"Th . . th . . th . ." he said, clutching hold of Thomas.

Thomas looked up from his book.

"What's the matter?" he asked. "You look as though you've seen a ghost."

"I . . I . . have . ." said Minty. "It's sw . . sw . . swimming in the river."

"Ghosts don't swim," laughed Thomas.

"Y . . yes they do!" said Minty. "I've seen one."

Wilbur went to see for himself and came back looking as scared as Minty.

"Minty's right," he said, "They do . ."

"Are you two playing a joke with me?" asked Thomas.

They shook their heads.

"Then I'd better take a look myself," said Thomas.

"It's over there!" they said, pointing the way but not attempting to move from where they stood. They waited for Thomas to gasp, for Thomas to turn pale. Instead, he laughed.

"It's not funny," said Wilbur. "We're frightened."

"What? Of a towel?"

"A towel!"

"Haven't you noticed? The one Minty pegged out earlier has blown away."

"If it's a towel, why is it moving like that?" asked Minty.

"Because it's wrapped itself round a duck."

Thomas called to the duck. "Can we have our towel back, please?"

But by that time, the duck was thoroughly frightened. She couldn't see anything. She couldn't hear anything properly either. Thomas's shouts frightened her even more.

"SQUAWK! SQUAWK! SQUAWK!" She was fluttering about like a bird caught in a net.

"Hold on," laughed Thomas. "I'll come and untangle you." He dived in and swam towards her.

"SQUAWK! SQUAWK!" The duck could hear Thomas coming, though she didn't know who it was, of course. One thing she did know and that was, no one . . . NO ONE . . . was going to catch HER.

He tried hard, but try as he did, Thomas just could not get close enough to her to pull the towel from her back.

"Keep away from me!" she squawked. "KEEP AWAY!"

Fergus Frog was sitting on the bank fishing.

"I wish you'd all go and play somewhere else," he shouted crossly. "You're disturbing the fish."

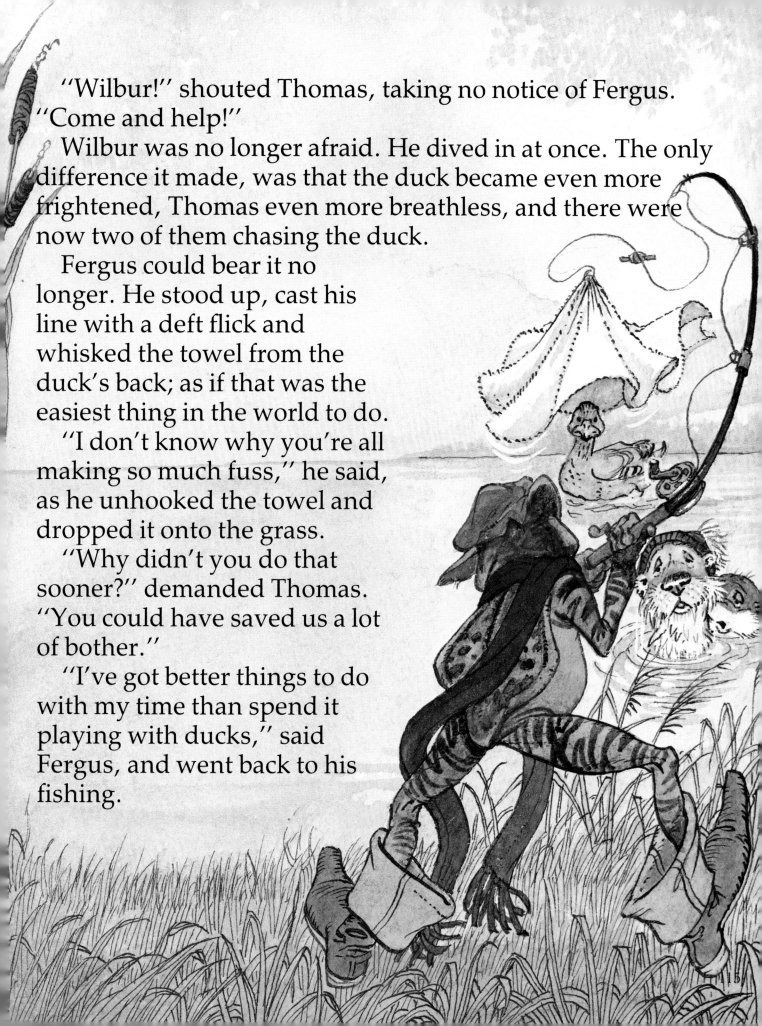

"Wilbur!" shouted Thomas, taking no notice of Fergus. "Come and help!"

Wilbur was no longer afraid. He dived in at once. The only difference it made, was that the duck became even more frightened, Thomas even more breathless, and there were now two of them chasing the duck.

Fergus could bear it no longer. He stood up, cast his line with a deft flick and whisked the towel from the duck's back; as if that was the easiest thing in the world to do.

"I don't know why you're all making so much fuss," he said, as he unhooked the towel and dropped it onto the grass.

"Why didn't you do that sooner?" demanded Thomas. "You could have saved us a lot of bother."

"I've got better things to do with my time than spend it playing with ducks," said Fergus, and went back to his fishing.

15

As soon as the duck could see where she was going, she swam off into the reeds and hid. She wouldn't come out until Thomas had explained about the towel.

"I've been rather silly, haven't I?" she said, turning a delicate shade of pink, and bowing her head shyly.

"I wouldn't say that," said Thomas kindly.

"I would!" shouted Fergus. "A lot of fuss about nothing, if you ask my opinion!"

"But we didn't," said Wilbur.

"And we're not going to, either," said Minty.

"I wouldn't tell you if you did," retorted Fergus.

"You already have!" sighed Thomas.

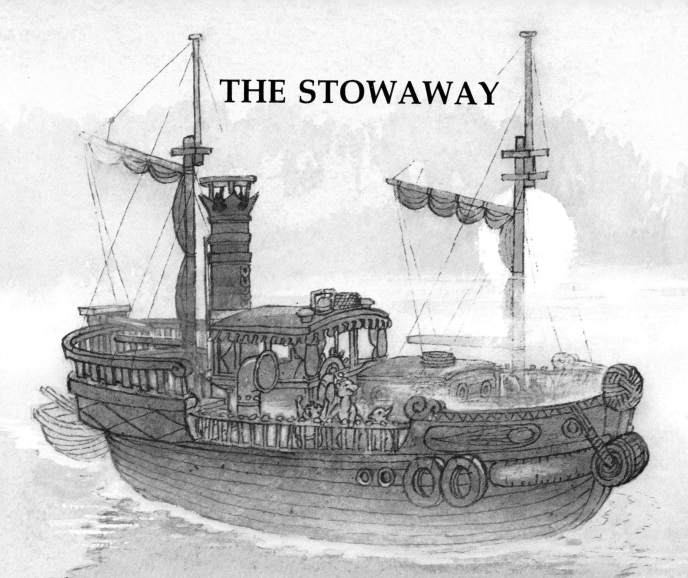

THE STOWAWAY

The sun was just breaking through the early morning mist and everyone aboard the Riverboat Tulip was waking up. Thomas went up on deck to look at the sky.

"It's going to be a nice day," he said, as Wilbur and Minty joined him. Then, someone coughed.

"Who was that?" asked Thomas, looking first at Wilbur and then at Minty. "Is one of you catching cold?"

"It wasn't me," said Wilbur.

"Or me," said Minty.

"And it wasn't me," said Thomas. "So WHO was it?" Once more they heard the sound of coughing.

"I can see someone in the dinghy," said Wilbur.

"Whoever you are, come out!" said Thomas sternly.

As they watched, there was a movement in the dinghy and the face of a mole looked up at them.

"I didn't mean any harm," said the mole, in a sad voice. "But I was so tired I just had to sleep. I didn't think you would mind."

"Well you're wrong!" shouted Minty. "We do mind! You've no business sleeping in our dinghy! It isn't a bed!"

"Shush" said Thomas gently. "Can't you see the poor little thing is ill? The sooner we get him on board the better."

Thomas got down into the dinghy. The little mole was shivering and shaking. His eyes were dull, his fur straggly and his whiskers limp.

"Please sir, I'm sorry," he said, shrinking away from Thomas. "I'll go straight away . . . please don't throw me into the river." His eyes were big and frightened as he tried to back away from Thomas.

"You're coming on board, whether you like it or not," said Thomas. "And there's no use in arguing." Then, to prove it, he lifted the mole up towards Minty and Wilbur, and they in their turn, lifted him aboard Tulip.

"You ARE a sad little thing," said Minty as the mole stood shivering and shaking before them. His knees were knocking and his teeth chattering. His fur was damp and was sticking to him like a wet coat. He looked very thin.

"No wonder he's coughing," said Wilbur. "He has hardly enough fur to keep him warm during the day, let alone during the night, and it was a cold night last night."

119

They took the mole below and wrapped him in a blanket. They gave him some hot soup in a mug.

"Now," said Thomas kindly. "Tell us what happened to you. Why were you in our dinghy?"

"I've caught a cold," said the little mole, and burst into another fit of coughing. "I don't know where it came from, but I've caught it . . . and it won't go away."

"Colds are like that," said Thomas. "Why aren't you tucked up in your own bed?"

"I was on my way home to do just that, but my head was aching and I couldn't remember which way to go. You see, I felt so poorly . . . and it was so cold . . . and when I saw your dinghy, I just climbed into it and went to sleep."

The little mole drank the hot soup and handed back the mug.

"I'll be going now," he said.

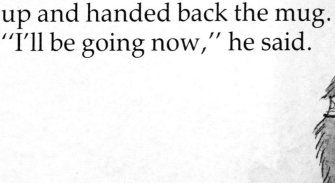

"No you won't," said Thomas firmly. He put a thermometer into the mole's mouth. "You have a very high temperature," he said when he took it out. "You are not going anywhere until you are well again." Then Thomas put the mole to bed in his own bunk.

The little mole didn't stir from the bunk for two whole days. Every time they tiptoed past him he was asleep. Thomas had to roll himself in a blanket and sleep on the cabin floor at night.

"The mole is sleeping a lot," said Wilbur as he tiptoed about in the galley.

"I expect he needs to," said Minty, with tears in his eyes. He had peeled an onion to make soup for the mole when he woke and that had made his eyes water.

On the third day, the little mole woke up. He sat up and said, brightly, "I'm hungry!" His eyes were clear and shining.

"Have some soup," said Minty. The mole spooned his way through three bowls of soup.

"Have some bread," said Wilbur. The mole nibbled his way through four thick slices.

"Do you feel better?" asked Thomas when the mole wiped his mouth and at last said he had had enough.

"Where did he put it all?" asked Wilbur in amazement.

Minty pointed to the mole's tummy. It was very round. VERY round indeed. "THAT'S where!" he said.

"Do you feel like getting up?" asked Thomas.

The little mole pushed back the covers and swung his feet over the side of the bunk. He stood up and carefully tried his legs.

"I'm as good as new," he said, with a smile that was as bright as the sunshine. "That horrid cold has quite . . . quite gone."

"Where do you suppose it went?" asked Minty, but no one answered.

It was hard to believe that this was the same mole they had found in the dinghy three days earlier. He was so cheerful and bouncy, so full of life. He kept making them laugh with the funny things he said and did.

They felt quite sad when they waved him goodbye. He went off with a map tucked under his arm. Over his shoulder, he carried some cheese and fruit wrapped in a cloth and tied to a stick.

"I wish he could have stayed longer," sighed Wilbur.

"We all do," said Thomas.

THE STORM

One night, when he was asleep, Minty rolled out of bed. He hit the floor with a bump and woke up.

"I wonder why I did that?" he said to himself, as he climbed back into his bunk. He was still wondering, when it happened again. This time Wilbur rolled out of HIS bunk. He hit the floor at the same time as Minty.

"How did that happen?" asked Wilbur when he had overcome his surprise, and they had untangled themselves.

Minty didn't answer. He was listening to something. "What's that noise I can hear?" he asked.

"The wind," said Thomas, who had been woken by all the goings on. "What are you two doing out of bed?"

"We rolled out," said Wilbur.

Thomas laughed. "You should have tucked yourselves in more tightly," he said. Then Tulip herself seemed to roll, and much to Thomas's surprise he found himself on the floor beside Minty and Wilbur.

"Listen to the wind," said Minty nervously. "It sounds angry to me." The wind was howling and whistling. The more it howled and whistled the more Tulip pitched and rolled. Wilbur stood up, and promptly fell down again. They could hear things sliding about in the galley. Something unseen fell with a crash. Over their heads they could hear things sliding about on deck.

"What's happening?" asked Minty. He was afraid, so he had hidden himself under the bunk.

A roll of thunder rumbled in the distance.

"There's a storm coming," said Thomas. "We'll have to go up on deck and fasten everything down or it will be swept into the river."

Out on deck they could feel the force of the wind. There was a very real danger that they would be taken off their feet by it and swept into the sky. Before they did anything at all, Thomas tied them all to safety lines. If the worst happened, there would be something to pull them back with. Then they got to work. The first thing they did was pull the dinghy on board.

Every time the lightning flashed across the dark sky they could see the trees along the riverbank swaying and bending with the wind. Tulip was bucking like a wild horse. But they were too busy to be frightened. They took below everything they could, and tied down everything else.

The wind seemed to grow wilder, the lightning brighter, and the thunder louder. Then when they had almost finished, the rain came.

It wasn't ordinary rain. The raindrops were as big as peas and as close together as peas inside a pod. It soaked them, and everything else, in an instant. It ran in solid sheets across the deck. It stung their faces . . . it hurt their ears.

"Get below!" ordered Thomas. "I'll finish here . . . Do as I say . . . GET BELOW!"

127

Minty and Wilbur fell down the stairway and were followed by a stream of water.

"THOMAS! THOMAS!" they shouted, fearful that they would never see him again. It seemed a long time before he came. They were so pleased to see him when he did, they hugged him tight, and almost cried.

Thomas shut the door and sat on the steps of the stairway. He looked very tired.

"There's nothing else we can do," he said. "We'll have to sit it out."

The storm raged for hours. But at last the rain stopped. The thunder became a soft rumble far away in the distance. The wind stopped howling. Tulip stopped pitching. And then they all fell asleep where they sat, too weary to even climb into their bunks.

THE FLOOD

The next morning when they woke, everything was quiet and still. They stretched their stiff limbs and went up on deck, to see how much damage had been done.

They stared, open-mouthed with dismay, at what they saw. The river had broken its banks. There was water EVERYWHERE. There wasn't a blade of grass to be seen. The hedges had almost disappeared and the trees had water halfway up their trunks.

And everywhere . . . EVERYWHERE . . . there were animals who had never climbed before, sitting in the branches of trees and on the tops of hedges.

There was no time to lose. "Wilbur, come with me!" said Thomas. "Minty, you prepare hot drinks and have towels ready."

Thomas and Wilbur lowered the dinghy and rowed to the nearest tree, where a family of rabbits were stranded.

Wilbur hung onto a branch to keep the dinghy steady.

"Young ones first," said Thomas. "Hand them down to me."

The rabbits huddled close together in the dinghy and shivered.

"Thank you . . thank you . ." said Mother Rabbit, as Thomas took them back to Tulip. "I don't think we could have held on much longer."

Minty helped the rabbits aboard and Thomas and Wilbur set off again.

Thomas and Wilbur rowed out eight times before everyone was rescued and safe on board Tulip. Well, almost everyone.

"I don't need rescuing," grumbled Owl as Wilbur tried to help him aboard the dinghy. Wilbur thought at first, he was afraid to jump. "Let go of my tail!" grumbled Owl. "This is my home . . . just you rescue everyone else so that I can have my home to myself again."

"Sorry," said Wilbur. "I didn't know."

"Well, you know now," said Owl, and then he winked to show that he wasn't cross at all.

Wilbur and Thomas were just about to climb aboard Tulip themselves for a well earned rest, when Minty stopped them. He pointed to a distant tree.

"There's someone over there," he said.

As the dinghy drew closer to the tree, Wilbur and Thomas saw something glint in the sun.

"I don't believe it," said Thomas. "It's a bicycle."

"Then it's safe to say Fergus is around here somewhere," sighed Wilbur.

"He's not in the tree," said Thomas.

"Of course I'm not. Why would I want to get into a tree?" Fergus was in the water beside them, idly paddling his long legs. "I wondered when you would get round to me."

"YOU don't need rescuing," said Wilbur. "You can swim. A flood is like a holiday to you."

"Maybe it is . . . but it's not a holiday for my bicycle."

"You don't really expect us to rescue your bicycle do you?" Thomas couldn't believe what he was hearing.

"Of course I do . . . move over . . . I'm coming in." Fergus hooked one leg over the side of the dinghy and pulled himself aboard.

"How did your bicycle get into the tree?" asked Thomas.

"I put it there," said Fergus.

Wilbur and Thomas exchanged looks.

"Put it there?" said Thomas. "Are you joking?"

"Of course not. I did put it there. It couldn't climb there by itself."

"But HOW did you get it up there?" asked Wilbur.

"With a great deal of difficulty," said Fergus, and he sighed as he remembered just HOW difficult it had been.

It was just as hard to get it down again, because not only had Fergus put the bicycle in the tree, he had tied it to the tree as well.

"Well, I didn't want it to fall out, did I?" he said to Wilbur and Thomas.

"What kind of knots are these?" asked Wilbur as he struggled to undo one.

"Frog's knots, of course," said Fergus. "What else would a frog use?"

"Ask a silly question," thought Thomas and smiled to himself.

When the last knot was untied, they lowered the bicycle into the dinghy and rowed back to Tulip.

"I might have guessed it would be you," said Minty, as they drew alongside.

"I don't know what you mean," said Fergus. "Clear a space . . . I don't want anyone near my bicycle."

"There isn't room for it," said Thomas. "It will have to stay in the dinghy."

"Then I'm staying with it," said Fergus. He did just that. He sat with his back to Tulip and took no notice of anyone. They were all amused.

By midday the flood water had soaked away and the grass was showing through. Everything steamed in the hot midday sun, and soon there were only puddles left.

Fergus and his bicycle were first ashore.

Wilbur couldn't resist calling after him. "Learn some new knots before you tie up your bicycle again."

"Huh!" said Fergus, as he rode off, carefully going round all the puddles. "YOU don't know a good knot when you see one, that's YOUR trouble!"

135

After Fergus had departed, Thomas took everyone else ashore and then, there was time and space to see what damage had been done to Tulip.

Everything could be put right again easily enough, but there was a great deal of clearing up to be done.

"We've had a lucky escape," said Thomas, as he reached for a mop and bucket.

"And so did everyone else," said Minty.

"And that includes a bicycle that belongs to someone we all know," laughed Wilbur. "'Frogs knots' indeed . . . whoever heard of anything so silly!"

STOP THIEF!

The next time they saw Fergus, he didn't have his bicycle with him. He was limping along the towpath, as though he had blisters on all his toes and creaks in all his joints. He was staring at the ground as though he was looking for something.

"Where's your bicycle?" called Minty.

"If I knew that, do you think I'd be walking?" said Fergus without looking up.

"Has something happened to it?" asked Minty.

"Perhaps he's tied it to a tree and forgotten where the tree is," giggled Wilbur.

"It's disappeared." Fergus sounded upset. "I only left it for a moment . . . someone has taken it."

"But that's not fair," said Minty. "They shouldn't have done that."

"Can we take you anywhere?" asked Thomas. Fergus wasn't used to walking.

"No, thank you," said Fergus. He wasn't usually so polite: it showed how upset he was. "I'm looking for clues. I don't want to miss anything."

They promised to keep a look-out for any sign of Fergus's bicycle and then they left him to his search for clues. They were all very quiet. They couldn't help thinking how forlorn he looked without his bicycle.

"I think we should go back and help him," said Minty presently, as he and Wilbur sat on deck shelling peas.

"We'd make too many footprints," said Wilbur. "We would cover up any clue that was there . . . and that wouldn't be helping at all."

"LOOK!"

Wilbur jumped up so suddenly the bowl of peas overturned and peas rolled all over the deck. "LOOK! That's Fergus's bicycle! I know it is! Stop! STOP THIEF!"

They shook their fists and shouted, but it was just a waste of time. The weasel who was riding Fergus's bicycle along the towpath, looked over his shoulder at them and smirked. He then pedalled harder than ever, hurtling along the towpath like a mini-rocket. He went over all the bumps and down all the potholes, without regard for Fergus's bicycle at all.

Minty and Wilbur raced up the wheelhouse steps two at a time, both shouting at once.

"Ferg . . . Ferg . . . it's . . . it's . . . quick . . . do some . . . Ferg . . ."

"Hold on! Hold on!" Thomas had his head inside a cupboard. He hadn't heard all the shouts. "What's the matter? One at a time . . . please . . ."

They both gulped, they both took a deep breath, and they both started again, rattling out words like peas from a pea-shooter.

"Fergus . . ." said Minty.

"Bicycle . . ." said Wilbur.

"Yes?" said Thomas.

"We've . . ." said Minty.

"Seen it . . ." said Wilbur.

"Where?" asked Thomas.

"On the towpath . . ."

"There's a weasel . . ."

"Riding it . . ."

"Then we must stop him."

"We've tried . . ."

"We shouted . . ."

"He wouldn't . . ."

"Stop . . ."

"Which way did he go?"

"That way . . ."

"I've got an idea!" said Thomas.

Thomas turned Tulip's engine to full-ahead. Tulip fairly flew through the water with the spray flying round her bow. They drew level with the weasel and passed him.

"Why did we do that?" asked Wilbur, as they turned a bend in the river and the weasel disappeared from view. "That's not helping . . . and we promised we would."

"That's running away without doing anything," said Minty.

Thomas was too busy to explain to them. He was steering Tulip straight into the bank. She came to a stop so suddenly that they were thrown off their feet.

"FOLLOW ME!" shouted Thomas, and leapt ashore.

"I wish we knew what we were doing," puffed Wilbur, as he and Minty followed behind.

"Pile those rocks on the path! QUICKLY!"

"Won't that be rather dangerous? Someone might fall over them."

"DO AS I SAY AND DO IT QUICKLY!"

They did as they were told. They had no choice. As they put the last rock in place, the weasel came whizzing round the corner on Fergus's bicycle. He saw the rocks but he was going too fast to stop. He hit them with a crunch. He was thrown right over the handlebars into a patch of brambles. The bicycle fell to the path with a clatter.

The sly weasel ran off with so many thorns sticking in him, he looked like a pin cushion.

Thomas picked up the bicycle. The front wheel was badly bent.

"Fergus is going to be very cross about that," sighed Wilbur. "He's going to say it was our fault."

But Fergus wasn't cross at all. He had seen everything as it happened, from the top of the hill. When he had seen the weasel with his bicycle, he thought he had lost it forever.

"I really am very grateful," he said. "And so are my legs," he added, as he rode off along the towpath with the bent wheel going bumpety-hop . . . bumpety-hop . . . "A frog's legs aren't made for walking."

THE CLOUD

"I hope we're not going to have another storm," said Minty looking anxiously at the sky. There was a large cloud gathering in the distance.

"It's coming this way," said Wilbur, and began dashing about covering everything up, just in case.

"There aren't any other clouds about," said Minty, still looking at the sky.

"Perhaps not, but that one there is getting much closer," said Wilbur. "Don't stand there staring at it. Come and help me."

Thomas heard them rushing about and came to see what they were doing.

"There's a great big cloud . . . it's going to rain," said Wilbur. "We're covering everything up."

"Doesn't look like a rain cloud to me," said Thomas.

"It's moving fast," said Minty.

"It's coming this way," said Wilbur.

"I don't know how," said Thomas. "There isn't any wind."

"There must be a wind, clouds don't move by themselves," said Wilbur.

"That one is," said Thomas. "It is not dark enough for a rain cloud."

"It's making a noise," said Minty presently. "I didn't know clouds could make noises."

The cloud came closer and the noise grew louder.

"Flp . . flp . . flp . ." it seemed to be saying, over and over again. And mixed in with the Flp . . flp . . flp . . was "Squk . . squk . . squk . ."

"There's GOT to be something wrong with my ears," said Minty.

"If there is something wrong with YOUR ears then there is something wrong with MINE," said Wilbur.

"It's a flock of birds," said Thomas suddenly. "A great big flock of birds."

Minty and Wilbur could see for themselves now. The birds were flying wing to wing, and tail to beak. They were all talking at once.

"Where are you all going?" called Thomas, as the leader of the flock passed over his head.

The bird inclined its head and looked down its beak.

"To warmer climes . . ." it said grandly. "We winter abroad, you know."

"You'd better look where you're going then," called Wilbur, "or you'll crash-land on your beak."

"You don't know very much do you?" said the bird with a superior smile.

The cloud of birds flew right over Tulip. It seemed to shut out the sun and cast a deep shadow across Tulip and the river. The birds' wings made so much wind, they raised the surface of the river in choppy waves. Wilbur and Minty, both being on the small side, had to grab hold of Thomas to stop themselves being swept overboard.

"This is almost as bad as being in a storm!" shouted Wilbur, as they stood together and stared upwards at the flapping wings.

"Don't you be cheeky down there," honked one of the birds, "or we will carry you off with us." It swooped down and pretended to put out its claws to pick up Wilbur. Wilbur screeched. He hid his face against Thomas and held on to him so tightly, Thomas could hardly breathe.

"Don't let him take me . . . please . . ." mumbled Wilbur.

"He wouldn't dare! Would he?" said Minty, hanging on to Thomas like a limpet himself.

"Of course not, he's teasing," laughed Thomas. "He wouldn't get very far carrying you, would he? He'd have to put you down pretty soon, or he'd get left behind himself."

"Has he gone?" asked Wilbur in a muffled voice. He didn't dare look himself.

"He has," said Thomas. "It's safe to come out."

It seemed to be a long time before the last of the birds passed over Tulip and the sun came out again.

"We'll see you on the way back!" called the last bird, as he dipped his wings and rolled in a goodbye salute.

"It isn't something I'll look forward to," said Wilbur.

"If I see them coming, I shall go below and lock myself in the galley till they've gone," said Minty.

"It wasn't as bad as all that," laughed Thomas. "I thought it was rather exciting. Now, who is going to sweep up all those stray feathers? There are enough there to make a pillow."

SURPRISE!

Wilbur and Minty had been on a secret mission ashore. They wouldn't tell Thomas where they were going. And when they came back, they wouldn't tell Thomas where they had been. They wouldn't tell him what was in the parcel they tried to hide behind their backs.

"What parcel?" they said, as if there was nothing there at all. They took it below and hid it beneath one of the bunks.

When they found Thomas sweeping in the cabin, they took the broom and bundled him out.

"We'll do that!" they said. "There must be plenty of things you can do in the wheelhouse."

Thomas saw the parcel in the galley, two days later, when Wilbur and Minty called to tell him breakfast was ready. It was sitting beside his plate, wrapped in brown paper and tied round with string.

"What's this?" he asked.

"It's for you!" said Wilbur and Minty together. "Happy Birthday, Thomas!"

"Is it really my birthday?" said Thomas.

"You know it is," laughed Minty. "No one forgets his own birthday." But Thomas really had forgotten.

"Undo it," said Minty.

"We hope you like it," said Wilbur.

They could hardly wait. They watched as Thomas first untied the string and rolled it up, then carefully removed the brown paper.

A beautiful smile lit up his face when he saw what was in the parcel. It was a squeeze-box accordion.

"Do you like it?" asked Minty and Wilbur.

"It's the best present anyone ever had," said Thomas and played a few notes.

"There . . . I told you he would know how to play it," said Minty happily.

"I've wanted one of these ever since I was knee-high to a grasshopper," said Thomas.

"You must have been very small when you were young," said Wilbur in amazement.

"I was," said Thomas.

After breakfast was eaten Wilbur and Minty sent Thomas up on deck to practise.

"We'll do the chores today," they said. "We want today to be a special day for you."

When the chores were done, they both sat in front of Thomas and watched him wiggle the squeeze-box in and out. They hugged themselves with delight.

Presently Thomas began to hum quietly as he played.

"Sing us a song," pleaded Minty.

Thomas knew lots of songs about the sea.

"If you join in with me," he said.

So they did. And when they'd sung that song, they sang another, then another, and another.

Presently, when they had finished one song and were deciding which one to sing next, there was a call from the bank. When they looked, they discovered they were not alone. Their friends had gathered on the riverbank and were listening.

"Don't stop singing!" they called. "We are enjoying ourselves!"

"So are we," called Thomas. "Why don't you come aboard and join in the singing?"

They didn't need inviting twice. Fergus was the first aboard. He pushed his bicycle up the gangplank and parked it beside the wheelhouse.

What a sing-song they had! Toes began to tap.

"Play us the sailors' hornpipe, Thomas!" called a rabbit when after a short time the singing came to an end.

"If Fergus will dance it for us," smiled Thomas.

Up jumped Fergus. His feet began to fly as Thomas squeezed out the hornpipe.

Faster and faster they went, till suddenly, without giving him any warning, Fergus's legs tied themselves into a figure eight and he had to stop. How everyone laughed.

"That's never happened before," he said looking down at his legs in surprise. "Will someone untie me?"

"Do you think that's a 'frog's knot'?" whispered Wilbur.

"It's a frog's legs tying it, so it must be," giggled Minty.

Thomas played the squeeze-box, and everyone else sang and danced, all the afternoon. When it began to get dark, Wilbur and Minty lit lanterns. Then, everyone sat, too tired to dance or sing but too happy and contented to move. Minty and Wilbur carried round trays of food and drinks and Thomas told one of his stories. It was the best birthday that Thomas had ever had.